Shu-Li
and
Diego

Shu-Li

By
Paul Yee

and Diego

Illustrated by
Shaoli Wang

Vancouver London

Published in 2009 in Canada and Great Britain by
Tradewind Books • www.tradewindbooks.com

Distribution and representation in Canada by
Publishers Group Canada • www.pgcbooks.ca

Distribution and representation in the UK by
Turnaround • www.turnaround-uk.com

Mixed Sources
Cert no. SW-COC-001271
© 1996 FSC
FSC

Inside pages printed on FSC certified paper using vegetable-based inks.

2 4 6 8 10 9 7 5 3 1
Printed in Canada

Cataloguing-in-Publication Data for this book
is available from The British Library.

Library and Archives Canada Cataloguing in Publication

Yee, Paul
Shu-Li and Diego / by Paul Yee ; illustrated by Shaoli Wang.

Sequel to Shu-Li and Tamara.
ISBN 978-1-896580-53-1

1. Dogs--Juvenile fiction. I. Wang, Shaoli, 1961- II. Title.

PS8597.E3S575 2009   jC813'.54   C2009-900913-7

For Robin and Jeff Cardozo-Richardson,
shining models for us all
—PY

For my angelic students
Stephanie, Silvia, Amelia, Winston and Ryan
—SW

The publisher acknowledges the support of the Canada Council for the Arts.

 Canada Council **Conseil des Arts**
for the Arts **du Canada**

The publisher also wishes to thank the Government of British Columbia for the financial support it has extended through the book publishing tax credit program and the British Columbia Arts Council.

BRITISH COLUMBIA
ARTS COUNCIL
Supported by the Province of British Columbia

The publisher also acknowledges the financial support of the Government of Canada through the Book Publishing Industry Development Program (BPIDP) and the Association for the Export of Canadian Books (AECB) for our publishing activities.

Chapter One

"Draw a picture of someone working. Make it someone you know," Mr. Ortega said. "Use black or coloured pencils. Have it ready to show to the class on Monday."

Thursday's homework had sounded simple enough, but Shu-Li Wu stared at her blank sheet of paper. *I'll never get this done on time*, she thought angrily.

She looked across the deli at her mother, who was posing for Shu-Li's classmate Diego. He had just put the finishing touches on his drawing. In the picture, Ma was standing behind the Yum Yum Deli counter, smiling broadly and holding out an almond cookie.

"Wow," Shu-Li exclaimed. "That's awesome!"

Shu-Li had never seen Diego's artwork before. Now she felt really discouraged.

I wish I was that good at art, she thought.

"I'm finished! I'm finished!" Tamara shouted. She was Shu-Li's best friend. She came running in from the kitchen holding a picture of Shu-Li's father. It showed Ba swinging a metal scoop full of steaming hot noodles.

"Now Tamara's all done too," Shu-Li moaned to herself.

"Whoa! Look at Diego's drawing," Tamara called out. "He's a real pro!"

Shu-Li glanced over and thought, *Great, they didn't leave anyone for me to draw.*

"Looks just like me," Ma said, pointing at Diego's picture.

"You can have it," Diego said, smiling. "I'll draw my father."

"Thank you," Ma said. "It's nice."

Just then the front door opened, and a dog with curly tan hair and big brown eyes bounded in.

"Baxter!" shouted Shu-Li.

The dog ran up to her, wagging his stubby tail.

"Mr. Simpson!" Ma exclaimed. "I tell you many times please do not bring dog here. He scare my customer."

Mr. Simpson owned the building the Yum Yum Deli was in. But Ma never minced words. She spoke her mind.

"I'm sorry," Mr. Simpson said. He ran his fingers through his hair and sighed. "I forgot."

"You need to talk? Tie Baxter outside," Ma said.

"Ah-rooo, rooooh!" the dog howled, suddenly jumping up at Tamara.

"Aagh!" she screamed. Backing away, she knocked over a chair.

"Don't be a fraidy-cat!" Shu-Li scoffed at Tamara. "There's nothing to be scared of!"

"Shu-Li, don't laugh at your friend," Ma said sternly.

"He's just being friendly," Mr. Simpson said, pulling at his dog's collar.

But Baxter lunged at Tamara again. With a yelp, she turned and ran out of the deli.

"I have to go into Mount Saint Joseph Hospital tomorrow for an operation," Mr. Simpson said to Ma, "and I'll be there for a week. Do you think Shu-Li could feed Baxter and take him for walks? I'll pay her. Mrs. Rossi offered to help, but she had to fly to Toronto at the last minute."

"Please, Ma," Shu-Li said, pressing her hands together. "I love Baxter!"

"She too busy with homework," Ma said to

Mr. Simpson, shaking her head. "Taking care of dogs is lots of work."

"But I can handle it, Ma," Shu-Li pleaded.

"You know nothing about dogs," Ma said. "They lots of trouble."

"Oh, Ma!" Shu-Li stamped her foot.

"You should ask Joey Zhang," Ma said to Mr. Simpson. "His family has a dog. He'll know about how to take care of Baxter."

"Where is Joey? He usually comes to the deli after school, doesn't he?" asked Mr. Simpson, looking around.

"He's got detention today," Shu-Li answered. "But he won't be able to do it, anyway. He sees a tutor after school Mondays and Tuesdays. And he practises break-dancing on Wednesdays."

"I can help," Diego called out. "We used to have a dog, but he ran away."

"Baxter is very well-behaved. He won't be

any trouble at all," Mr. Simpson said. "How about it, Mrs. Wu?"

"Shu-Li too busy," Ma protested.

"All they have to do is walk and feed him," Mr. Simpson argued. "Please, Mrs. Wu? It's too late for me to find anyone else. I wouldn't ask you if I didn't think Shu-Li could handle it."

"Oh, all right," Ma replied with a smile. "I tell Ba."

"Here's a spare key to my house," said Mr. Simpson, handing it to Ma.

He turned to Shu-Li and Diego. "Start tomorrow after school. Take Baxter for a long walk and feed him when you get back. After that, you'll need to walk him twice a day— before and after school. I'll leave out all the dog food he'll need and some baggies to scoop up his poop."

Poop! Shu-Li shuddered. *Yuck!*

Chapter Two

The next day after school, Shu-Li and Diego took Baxter to Grandview Park.

"Give me the leash," Diego commanded.

"But Baxter knows me better," Shu-Li protested.

Diego grabbed the leash anyway and ran ahead.

"Baxter is *my* friend!" Shu-Li shouted. "Mr. Simpson asked *me* to walk him!"

Suddenly Baxter stopped. Shu-Li ran over and pulled the leash away from Diego. "Don't let him eat junk off the street!"

"Pizza crust is okay."

"No, it's not!" Shu-Li grabbed the crust and tossed it into a nearby garbage can.

When she turned around, Baxter was making a huge poop. "Yuck," she said, pinching her nose. "You need to clean that up."

"Not me! You have the leash."

"I've never done it. Show me how to do it."

"Okay. But you have to do it the next three times we take him out for a walk."

"Three times? That's not fair!"

"You need the practice."

Shu-Li made a face at Diego as he pulled out a baggie. He scooped the poop with one quick move and tossed it into the garbage can.

"Go, boy," Shu-Li said, removing Baxter's leash. "Go get some exercise."

"Hey!" Diego shouted. "You can't let dogs off the leash here. See that sign?"

Baxter was already running across the park.

"Stop!" Shu-Li shouted. "Come back!"

As Baxter raced toward the flower garden, Diego sprinted across the grass after him.

"Come back!" Shu-Li shouted again.

Baxter tore up a flowerbed before he could be stopped.

"Diego!" Constable Jane Rooney braked hard on her bike. "What does that sign say?"

"All dogs must be kept on leash," he answered, pulling Baxter out of the flowers. "But it's not my fault, Constable. Shu-Li let him go."

Shu-Li's face turned red. "I didn't know the rule," she said, looking down and clipping the leash back onto Baxter's collar.

When she looked up, Shu-Li's heart sank.
Three girls from her class were standing behind
Constable Rooney, smirking at Shu-Li and
Diego. They wore fancy sunglasses and had
their arms crossed over their chests. They called

themselves the *Nah-Nah Girls*.

"Look at all the broken flowers!" Hannah cried out, pretending to be shocked.

"What a mess!" exclaimed Shona.

Jenna scrunched up her face, wagged her finger and made tut-tut noises between her teeth.

"Pick up all the broken flowers before the gardeners get here," Constable Rooney said. "And be more careful the next time you take Baxter on a walk."

Then she rode off and the *Nah-Nah Girls* went away, much to Shu-Li's relief.

Shu-Li tied Baxter to a bench. Then she and Diego picked up the broken flowers and dumped them into a garbage can.

"Don't say anything to my mother or there'll be big trouble," she said to Diego.

• • •

"Paco was the best dog," Diego said when they had finished cleaning up.

"Do you miss him?"

"Remember how he used to stand up on his hind legs?" he asked.

"Did you ever draw pictures of him?"

He shook his head.

"Will you ever get another dog?"

"I sure hope so. I want a dog more than anything in the world."

"So do I."

"My father blames me for Paco running away. But maybe if he sees what a good job I'm doing with Baxter, he'll get me another dog."

"Was it really your fault?"

Diego didn't answer.

• • •

On the way out of the park, they saw Tamara sitting alone on a bench.

"Hey!" called Shu-Li, waving her hand.

A squirrel dashed up a tree, and Baxter leaped after it, dragging Shu-Li behind him. But Diego grabbed the leash and pulled him back.

When Shu-Li looked over at the bench, Tamara was gone.

Chapter Three

On Saturday morning, Shu-Li met Diego at
Mr. Simpson's house.

"Let's go visit Mr. Simpson at Mount Saint
Joseph," Diego suggested. "He must need
cheering up. We can surprise him."

"Do you know where the hospital is?"

"Sure. My father works there."

"Is he there today?"

"No, it's his day off."

"Ma will never let me go," Shu-Li said,
shaking her head.

"We just won't tell her," Diego said, grinning.

Shu-Li had never visited a hospital before. She had seen one on TV, and it had looked scary, full of sick and dying people. Worse, she knew she would get into big trouble if Ma and Ba ever found out. *But I'm not a fraidy-cat*, she thought.

"Okay, okay," she said. "Let's take the bus."

"They don't let dogs on the bus. We can just walk."

"Walk? No way."

"It only takes half an hour. I've done it lots of times with my mother. Sometimes we meet my dad when he gets off work. Then the three of us go to Main Street to a Mexican restaurant that we like."

"Okay, we'll walk."

• • •

They went up Commercial Drive. At the corner of Broadway, lots of people were coming out of the Skytrain station.

Suddenly Baxter sat down and refused to move.

"Come on, Baxter! Don't be afraid. Come on, boy," Diego said.

"Maybe we should turn around and go home," Shu-Li said. "Baxter seems worried."

Diego reached down and scratched Baxter behind his ears.

"Ah-rooo, rooooh," Baxter cried out and stood up.

They turned right on Broadway and walked past Clark Drive and Vancouver City College. They hiked up the hill to Fraser Street.

They went past stores, car repair shops and restaurants. Shu-Li had never walked this far without Ma or Ba.

Baxter stopped dead in his tracks again. He was panting heavily and his long pink tongue hung out from his mouth.

"He's tired," Shu-Li said. "This is taking longer than you said. Do you really know where you're going?"

"Of course I do."

"It's been forty minutes already. You said half an hour. Let's ask for directions."

"We're almost there. The hospital is only a couple of blocks away."

"Right!" Shu-Li didn't believe him. *I should just jump on a bus and go home right now,* she thought.

"Look!" Diego pointed across the street. "A pet store. Maybe Baxter just needs some water."

A shiny bowl sat by the door, and Baxter lapped up the water.

Mount Saint Joseph Hospital stood on a quiet street just off Kingsway. Visitors walked past them carrying pots of flowers and stuffed animals.

"Can dogs go in?" Shu-Li whispered to Diego as they approached the entrance.

"Of course. People bring pets in all the time."

It was cool inside. Nurses wearing bright uniforms hurried by, pushing carts filled with medicines.

Suddenly Baxter growled, jerked free and ran down the hall chasing a tiny little dog. A nurse stepped out of a room, and Baxter almost knocked her over. She screamed and dropped her medicine tray, which fell to the floor with a clatter. The noise made Baxter run even faster. An elderly man in a wheelchair tried to avoid the charging dog and smashed into a wall. The two dogs chased one another down the hall and around the corner. Diego dashed after them.

Shu-Li stood frozen on the spot.

Chapter Four

After a couple of minutes, Diego came back empty-handed.

"Oh great! Now what?" Shu-Li asked.

"Ah-rooo, rooooh," Baxter cried out, hurtling toward them from the other end of the hall.

"Grab him!" Shu-Li yelled.

Diego lunged and grabbed Baxter's leash as the other dog dashed by.

"Now behave yourself," Diego warned. "We're in a hospital."

After Baxter settled down, they went in search of Mr. Simpson's room. When they found it, Baxter ran straight to the bed and barked, "Ah-roo, rooooh!" Then he jumped up and put his paws on Mr. Simpson's lap, panting loudly.

"Hey, boy," Mr. Simpson said weakly. "I missed you."

Baxter's long tongue darted out and licked his owner's face.

"Thanks for bringing him to visit me. Has he been any trouble?"

"Oh, no!" said Shu-Li. "No trouble at all."

"He's a great dog. And really well-behaved," Diego added.

The smile on Mr. Simpson's face lit up the room.

Shu-Li thought, *It's a good thing he doesn't know how much trouble Baxter caused!*

After taking Baxter home, Shu-Li hurried to the deli. As soon as she stepped in, she saw Constable Rooney at the counter talking to Ma.

"Where did you go?" Ma demanded, rushing up to Shu-Li. "I went looking for you."

Shu-Li couldn't speak. Her throat felt as dry

as paper. *Oh no!* she thought. *The hospital phoned.*
They're mad about Baxter running around!

"Your mother stopped me in the park and
asked me if I had seen you anywhere," the
police officer said.

"It was Diego's idea, not mine," Shu-Li blurted out.

"What idea?" Constable Rooney asked.

"To take Baxter to see Mr. Simpson."

"You go all the way to hospital?" Ma's eyes grew large.

Constable Rooney shook her head and said, "Next time you go anywhere, make sure you tell your parents."

"Sorry. So much trouble for you," Ma said to the officer. "Goodbye and thank you for your help." Then she turned to Shu-Li. "Just you wait till Ba get back from market." Her lips were tight with anger.

Shu-Li swallowed hard. "But it was Diego's idea, not mine."

"Think for yourself!" scolded Ma. "Never run off. Hospital is too far away."

"Mr. Simpson was really happy to see us. You should have seen his smile."

"Is he okay?"

Shu-Li nodded and said, "He's fine. He said he really missed Baxter."

"Never do this again," Ma said sternly. "I should punish you, but it was nice that you visit a sick man."

"So you won't tell Ba?" Shu-Li asked, holding her breath.

"Go to kitchen and do chores," Ma said, sighing. "Tamara came by. She say she not helping you any more."

"I know why she's upset. I haven't had any time for her."

Shu-Li went to the kitchen. A big pile of Chinese parsley was waiting. She washed her hands, put on an apron and began to pick the tender green leaves from the stalks.

Great! she thought miserably. *Now I have even more work to do. I should never have agreed to take care of Baxter.*

With Tamara's help, Shu-Li had always managed to do the chores quickly. Now Shu-Li missed laughing with her and talking about school. Too bad Tamara was afraid of dogs. If she wasn't so frightened, then she could have helped with Baxter too. Shu-Li remembered being scared of dogs when she was a little girl in China. There they seemed to jump and howl like wolves, showing rows of huge pointed teeth.

If I can lose my fear of dogs, she thought, *then so can Tamara.* Shu-Li decided to ask her to help them walk Baxter.

Chapter Five

Monday turned out to be a really bad day. In the morning, it was raining hard. Deep puddles were everywhere, and Baxter splashed through every one of them. When he shook himself dry, Shu-Li and Diego got soaked. So they each had to go back home and change their clothes, which made them late for school.

This was the day they were supposed to show their art to the class.

Shu-Li went up first. Last year when she was new at the school, she was scared to stand in front of the class and speak out. Now she had friends, so she didn't worry any more.

She held up her drawing.

"Is it a sheep?" one girl asked.

"A buffalo," another said.

"Is it a turkey, Mr. Ortega?"

"It's a dog and his name is Baxter Brown-Eyes," Shu-Li said nervously, wondering if her drawing was really that awful.

"But you were supposed to draw a person, not a pet," Mr. Ortega said.

"Baxter is Mr. Simpson's best friend. To him he's just like a real person," Shu-Li said.

"But the assignment was to draw someone

at work," Mr. Ortega insisted.

"Baxter has two jobs," Shu-Li answered. "His first is to make sure his owner, Mr. Simpson, goes for two walks every day. Baxter's other job is to be a watchdog. Whenever anyone comes near Mr. Simpson's house, Baxter barks like this. Ah-rooo, rooooh, rooooh!" Shu-Li howled long and high just like Baxter.

All the kids laughed. Mr. Ortega laughed too.

Then Diego went to the front of the room and held his drawing up. Everyone clapped.

"That's a doctor!" Joey shouted.

The picture showed a man wearing a lab coat with a stethoscope around his neck.

"That's my father," Diego said. "He's a doctor."

"No way!" Tamara called out.

Everyone turned to look at her.

"My mom works with Diego's father at Mount Saint Joseph. He's a nurse's helper."

"My father is so a doctor!" Diego insisted.

"He is not," replied Tamara.

Oh no! Shu-Li thought. *One of them is a liar!*

"The important thing is," Mr. Ortega said, "that Diego's father and Tamara's mother both work helping sick people."

When Tamara showed the class the picture she had drawn of Shu-Li's father, everyone recognized him.

"He's the owner of the Yum Yum Deli!" Satindar yelled.

After class, Shu-Li went over to Tamara.

"I liked your drawing of Ba," Shu-Li said. "It was great."

But Tamara shrugged her off without saying a word or even looking at her.

To make matters worse, Shu-Li couldn't find Diego. So she trudged off to Mr. Simpson's in the pouring rain.

When Shu-Li got back from walking Baxter, she was soaked for the second time that day. Diego stood waiting for her, nervously shuffling back and forth.

"Sorry, I had to help my mom, but I'll dry Baxter and feed him."

Shu-Li nodded and ran off.

"It's not so easy taking care of Baxter, is it?" Ma asked with a smile as Shu-Li entered the deli. "Do you still want a dog?"

"Oh yes!"

Ma frowned. "Dry your hair before you do your chores."

Shu-Li groaned when she saw the large sack of peanuts on the work counter. It would take at least an hour to shell them and remove all the peels.

She stamped her foot and thought, *I've got to find a way to make up with Tamara.*

She dried her hair and washed her hands. But before she could turn off the tap, Diego rushed in.

"Baxter ran away! I tied him to the railing on the porch to dry him off. And when I went into the house to get a towel, he ran off!"

They dashed out of the kitchen.

"Baxter ran away!" Shu-Li shouted.

"I told you dogs are trouble!" Ma exclaimed.

"We have to go look for him, right now!" Shu-Li said, grabbing her rain poncho.

"I already went around the block," Diego said. "But I didn't see him."

Shu-Li and Diego ran out the front door but stopped. Which way should they go?

"Did you check the alley?" Shu-Li asked. "Today is garbage day, and Baxter likes to sniff all the cans."

"Baxter, Baxter!" they called, running through the puddles. "Come here, boy!"

Chapter Six

The sky brightened and the rain stopped.
But Baxter wasn't in the alley or in any of the
nearby streets. Shu-Li and Diego peered under
porches and behind bushes. They went into
Grandview Park and checked the clubhouse,
the washrooms and the playground. Diego
whistled, but Baxter didn't come running.

"How could you be so stupid?" Shu-Li asked. "Are you sure you tied him up?"

"He slipped out of his collar!"

"Is that how you lost Paco?"

"Let's try the pet store," Diego said, glaring at her. "Maybe Mr. Kogawa can help."

They ran to the pet store.

"Mr. Kogawa, have you seen Baxter?" Shu-Li asked.

"Is he lost?"

"Yes," answered Diego.

"I'll call the SPCA shelter and see if anyone has turned him in," Mr. Kogawa said, picking up the phone. "If not, you can call the newspaper and put in a lost dog ad. Here's the number."

"Mr. Simpson will be so upset," Shu-Li said, bursting into tears.

"Don't worry. We'll find Baxter," Diego said.

"But you never found Paco."

Shaking his head, Mr. Kogawa put down the phone and said, "There's no trace of him at the shelter."

"Maybe Baxter went to the hospital looking for Mr. Simpson," Shu-Li said. "Can you try phoning there?"

Mr. Kogawa made the call while Shu-Li and Diego listened anxiously. "Baxter's not at the hospital either," Mr. Kogawa said. "But they'll call your mother if he turns up."

Shu-Li's hand jumped to her mouth as a terrible thought came to her, *What if Baxter got hit by a car?*

Mr. Kogawa continued. "Don't worry, someone will find him and read his dog tag."

"Umnn...Baxter slipped out of his

collar when I was washing him," Diego said nervously.

"You're so stupid," Shu-Li said to him. "Now what?"

"You better tell Mr. Simpson that Baxter ran away," Mr. Kogawa cautioned.

"But what if that makes him sicker?" Shu-Li asked.

"Hmm, that's a good point. You could wait till tomorrow to tell him. Baxter will probably show up by then."

"We made LOST DOG signs like those for Paco," Diego said, pointing at the posters pinned to the bulletin board. "But we had a photo of Paco and we don't have one of Baxter."

"You could draw a picture of Baxter, Diego," Shu-Li suggested.

"That's a great idea," Mr. Kogawa said. "I'll get paper and pencil crayons."

"No way," Diego said.

Diego crossed his arms over his chest.

"Why not?" Shu-Li asked. "You're great at drawing."

"You do it," he said, looking away. "You drew him for class. I can't draw from memory."

"No one will know what we're looking for if I draw Baxter."

"Why don't you give it a try?" Mr. Kogawa said to Diego, holding out the paper.

Diego didn't budge.

"If you don't try, I'll phone Mr. Simpson and tell him you lost his dog," Shu-Li said.

"You won't!"

"I will too!"

"Okay, okay." Diego grabbed a pencil crayon and started to draw.

"Make his ears shorter," Shu-Li ordered.

"Don't boss me around. I know what to do."

"Put the deli phone number on it."

"Shut up and let me draw!"

Diego spent the next fifteen minutes
working on the drawing with Shu-Li looking

over his shoulder. When he finished, he held up
the picture for Mr. Kogawa to see.

"That looks just like Baxter," Mr. Kogawa
said. "I'll make some copies, and you can put
them up all over the neighbourhood."

• • •

Shu-Li and Diego went up and down
Commercial Drive taping the posters up on
store windows, bus shelters, lamp posts and
newspaper boxes. They also dropped them off

at the Britannia Community Centre, the library and at every coffee house.

By the time they got back to the deli, it was dinnertime and the place was full of customers. The aroma of Ba's cooking made Shu-Li's stomach growl. But she was too upset to eat.

"I guess you didn't find Baxter," Ma said, looking at the poster that Shu-Li handed her.

"No, we didn't," Diego said.

"This is all your fault," Shu-Li said, pouting. "I should never have let you help me."

"Blaming me won't help us find him."

They stared at each other in stony silence.

"Shu-Li, you need to tell Mr. Simpson you lost his dog," Ma said.

"But someone will see the poster and call," Diego said.

"Mr. Kogawa said to wait till tomorrow before we tell Mr. Simpson," Shu-Li said.

"Is that so?" Ma said. "We'll see what Ba has to say about that!"

Chapter Seven

On Tuesday Shu-Li worried about Baxter all through class. Was he still alive? Was he stolen? Had he been injured?

"Shu-Li Wu! Shu-Li Wu!" called Mr. Ortega.

Shu-Li jumped out of her seat and stood at attention.

"Yes, Mr. Ortega?"

"Are you daydreaming, young lady? I asked you a question. Didn't you hear me?"

Her classmates turned around to stare.

"Uh, what was the question?" Her voice trembled.

"Never mind. Just sit down and make sure you pay attention."

Just before lunch, when the students were reading aloud one by one, Mr. Ortega called out, "Diego, it's your turn to read."

Diego didn't answer.

"What's the matter? Have you lost your place?"

His classmates turned around to stare.

Diego nodded.

"Please pay attention, young man!"

Then someone knocked at the classroom door.

Maybe it's the school secretary with a message, Shu-Li thought. *Maybe someone found Baxter!*

But it was just a note for Hannah.

At lunchtime, Shu-Li looked for Tamara and found her in the playground talking to Jenna and Shona. *Oh no!* Shu-Li thought, *Tamara has joined the Nah Nah Girls!* Dejected, she turned away.

Then Joey ran up and said he had seen the poster. "Did you really lose Baxter?" he asked.

Shu-Li nodded miserably.

"I'd help you look for him," Joey said, "if I didn't have to meet my tutor today."

After school, Shu-Li ran to the deli as fast as she could.

"Did anyone phone?" she shouted.

Ba shook his head. "You better look at this. A reporter saw your poster and put it on the front page of the paper." He held the newspaper up. Diego's drawing of Baxter was right below a big headline: GREAT ART FOR LOST DOG. Ba frowned. "When Mr. Simpson sees it, he'll know Baxter is missing. You and Diego better go to the hospital right now and tell everything to Mr. Simpson. I'll drive you there."

"But someone might see the newspaper and call us," Shu-Li said, stalling for time.

"We go now!"

"All right, I'll get Diego," she muttered.

Shu-Li trudged up the block. But when she knocked on the front door of Diego's house, no one answered. She waited and knocked again. She shouted his name. But no one came out.

"Oh, great, now I have to tell Mr. Simpson the bad news all by myself." She looked around, wishing that Baxter would come running. No such luck.

Back at the deli, Tamara was waiting.

"Shu-Li, are you okay?" her friend asked. "I saw the poster. This is awful!"

"Oh, Tamara," cried Shu-Li. Tears welled up in her eyes. "I'm so sorry. It was stupid of me to laugh when Baxter jumped on you. You're my best friend. I missed you."

Tamara bit her lip. After a pause, she said, "When I was little, a big dog bit me. Mom rushed me to the hospital for stitches."

"You should have told me," Shu-Li said. "You want to know a secret? I used to be scared of dogs too. That was when I was little in China. Guard dogs were everywhere. My father had to carry me past them."

"How did you stop being scared?"

"I met Baxter."

"Poor Baxter," Tamara said. "Do you think you'll find him?"

"We *have* to find him."

"What can I do to help?"

"Would you come to the hospital with me?"

"Where's Diego?" asked Tamara.

"I don't know. He's never around when I need him! Will you come?"

"Of course. What are friends for?"

Ba dropped the girls off at the hospital entrance. "Don't be long," he said. "I have to make food for customers. And tell Mr. Simpson I will drive

him home tomorrow. He should phone me
when he's ready to leave."

"Aren't you coming with us?" Shu-Li asked.

"No, it was your job to take care of the dog.
So you tell Mr. Simpson the truth."

Chapter Eight

As the girls walked into the hospital, Shu-Li was afraid somebody might recognize her as the girl who had let loose the wild dog. So she hid behind Tamara. But nobody paid any attention to them.

"Mr. Simpson," Shu-Li said, when they finally got to his room, "you look much better."

"Hey, Shu-Li. It's good to see you." He smiled. "Hey, Tamara, it's nice of you to visit. Did you bring Baxter?"

"Uh…no…uh…"

Tamara stepped on Shu-Li's toe, hard.

"Ow!" Shu-Li cried, glaring at her.

Just then a man in a green uniform arrived with Mr. Simpson's dinner.

"Hi, Mr. Castillo. Mr. Simpson, this is Diego's father." Shu-Li said.

"Hi, Shu-Li. Hi, Tamara," Mr. Castillo said. "Is Diego with you?"

"No. He took Baxter to the park for a walk," Shu-Li said. Then she added, "Diego sure loves dogs. He really enjoys being with Baxter. He would sure like another dog."

Tamara was so surprised that her mouth fell open.

"Mr. Castillo, are you a doctor?" Shu-Li asked, changing the subject.

"Yes. I earned my medical degree at San Carlos University in Guatemala. But in order to practise medicine here, I have to get certified." He smiled at her. "So I'm working at Mount Saint Joseph until I pass my exams."

So Diego was telling the truth, Shu-Li thought.

"I know a doctor from China who has to work as a waiter," Mr. Simpson said.

"You two should probably let Mr. Simpson eat his dinner," Mr. Castillo said.

"Okay. Bye, Mr. Simpson," Shu-Li said.

"Bye, Dr. Castillo," Tamara said.

"Ba says you should call him when you're ready to leave tomorrow," Shu-Li said. "He'll pick you up."

"Okay. Thank him for me and thanks for coming to visit. Tell Diego thanks for taking such good care of Baxter."

As they left the room, Tamara whispered, "What's the matter with you? Why didn't you tell him Baxter ran away?"

"Just don't tell Ba, okay?"

"Okay, but this wasn't my idea. Remember that!"

"Thanks. You're the best."

On the way home in the car, the girls were quiet.

"What did Mr. Simpson say?" Ba asked.

"He was upset," Shu-Li replied. "But he

said everyone in the city will see the poster in the newspaper, so he's sure someone will find Baxter."

"Yes, the dog can't be far away," Ba said.

Shu-Li imagined Mr. Simpson walking into an empty house and wondering where Baxter was. Then she imagined what Ba would do when he found out that she never told Mr. Simpson anything about Baxter.

At the deli, Diego was waiting for them.

"We saw your dad at the hospital," Shu-Li said. "You never told him about losing Baxter, did you?"

"No. Because then I'd never get another dog! Did you tell him about Baxter?"

"No. And she didn't tell Mr. Simpson either," Tamara said.

"We're done for now," Diego said.

"Your father told us he was a doctor before

coming to Canada," Tamara said. "Sorry about what I said in class."

"That's okay."

Ma brought over glasses of juice. "Children shouldn't look so sad," she said. "Cheer up. Maybe you go look for Baxter in the park."

"He won't be there," Diego said.

"It's better than sitting here and doing nothing," Tamara said.

"Maybe we should call the animal shelter again," Shu-Li suggested.

"Maybe we should go there and get Mr. Simpson another dog," Ma said.

"Mr. Simpson doesn't want another dog. He loves Baxter," Shu-Li said.

"But a new dog is better than no dog," Ma said.

Just then the telephone rang and Ma went

to answer it. When she came back she announced, "Some people found Baxter! They saw his picture in the newspaper. They'll bring him back tomorrow. I'll call Mr. Simpson and tell him. He'll be so happy."

"No! Don't call!" Shu-Li screamed. "I never told Mr. Simpson that Baxter was missing!"

Ma glanced toward the kitchen. "Ba will be so angry when he finds out," she said. "He drove you to the hospital just so you could tell Mr. Simpson what happened to Baxter."

"Do we have to tell him?" Shu-Li asked. "Baxter will be back tomorrow and Mr. Simpson won't even know he ran away."

"What if he saw the newspaper?" Ma asked.

The three kids looked at each other.

Chapter Nine

After school on Wednesday, Shu-Li, Tamara, Joey and Diego hurried to the deli to decorate it for Mr. Simpson's coming-home party. Shu-Li's parents had invited all the neighbours. Trays of food were set up inside, and Diego had hung up a banner that said WELCOME HOME MR. SIMPSON.

Shu-Li and Tamara climbed up on chairs and taped coloured streamers onto the front window.

"I hope Ma didn't say anything to Ba," Shu-Li said.

A car pulled up and parked in front. A man
got out leading a dog on a leash. It was Baxter.

Just then, Joey walked up and Baxter
jumped on him.

"Down, boy!" the man said, pulling hard on
Baxter's leash.

A woman carrying another dog came up
beside him, and they all walked into the deli.

"Hi, I'm Anil," the man said.

"I'm Yasmin and this is Raja," the woman said, patting her dog.

"Hi, I'm Shu-Li and this is Tamara and Joey."

"I'm Diego. I drew the picture of Baxter."

Then Ma came rushing over. "You must be Mr. and Mrs. Danini. I'm Mrs. Wu. We talk on the phone. How you find Baxter?"

"On Monday night, we came home from walking our dog and found Baxter shivering at our front door," Yasmin said. "He was dripping wet."

"We brought him inside and dried him off," Anil added. "Then we fed him some rice and lamb. He lay right down and fell asleep."

"That dog sure snores loud," Yasmin said, laughing.

"Where do you live?" Diego asked.

"In Mount Pleasant, near the hospital," Anil replied.

I was right about where he went, Shu-Li thought.

Shu-Li brought Tamara over to Baxter. "Let him smell the back of your hand. If he licks it, then you can gently pet him."

Tamara held out her hand and Baxter's long tongue slobbered all over it.

Just then, Tamara's mother arrived with a box of her famous Nanaimo bars, followed by Constable Rooney with a bag of her home-made doggie treats.

"Look, Mama. He likes me!" Tamara exclaimed.

Mr. Kogawa came in and slipped a brand new collar around

Baxter's neck with a bright green leash attached. "Welcome home gifts," he said.

Suddenly Baxter let out a loud, "Ah-rooo, rooooh, rooooh!"

Everyone looked out the window as Ba's car pulled up.

Officer Rooney went to help Mr. Simpson get out. He leaned on his cane and waved to everyone.

"Mrs. Wu, is it okay for dogs to come into the deli today?" Mr. Simpson asked with a smile, as he walked through the door.

"Of course," Ma exclaimed. "Everyone knows this is a party for you and Baxter."

Mr. Simpson sat down on a chair. Baxter laid his head on his owner's lap and sighed.

Then the newspaper reporter who wrote the article about Baxter came in.

"Uh-oh!" Shu-Li exclaimed.

"Now we're *really* done for," Diego said.

"Everyone stand together. I want to take a picture," the reporter said. "I'm writing a happy ending to this."

Shu-Li gulped and went over to Mr. Simpson. "I should have told you when I saw you at the hospital. Baxter got loose and ran away. We looked for him everywhere, but…"

"Don't worry about it," Mr. Simpson said, interrupting. "Your father told me everything. You kids did the best you could. If you hadn't put up the posters, Baxter might still be lost."

Shu-Li looked over at Ba, who smiled back.

Everyone gathered around Mr. Simpson and Baxter, and the reporter took their picture.

Then Diego's parents walked into the deli.

"Here, Diego," Mr. Castillo said, holding out a puppy. "He is for you because you took such good care of Baxter."

Diego was speechless as the puppy licked his face. Then he took a deep breath and said,

"Papa, Mama, you'd better take the puppy back. I didn't take such good care of Baxter. He ran away."

"But you did take good care of him," Mr. Simpson said. "It wasn't your fault he ran away. I should have thrown away that old collar of his."

"And look at the picture Diego drew," the reporter said, handing the newspaper to Mr. Castillo. "You must be proud."

"We certainly are!" Mrs. Castillo said.

"It's your puppy, Diego," Mr. Castillo said. "Next time, just don't be afraid to tell us when something goes wrong."

"Same thing goes for you, Shu-Li," Ba said.

"Okay, Ba," she said. "I will."

"What will you call him?" Mrs. Castillo asked, hugging Diego.

"I'll call him Paco."

"I'll help you walk him," Shu-Li said.

"Me too!" Tamara added.

Joey was too busy eating to say anything.

"Ah-rooo, rooooh!" Baxter howled. Paco and Raja joined in, barking and yelping.

Everyone laughed.

10 Top Dog Tips from Shu-Li and Diego

Exercise

1. Give your dog LOTS of exercise!

2. Walk your dog at the same time each day. Dogs like things to happen regularly.

Food

3. Don't over-feed. Your dog's heart will be healthier.

4. Once in a while, put something new into their meals. Try carrots or cheese. But check with your parents first.

5. Don't feed your dog when you are eating. You don't want a dog that begs for food.

Grooming

6. Brush your dog's teeth at least twice a week.

7. Make sure your dog's toenails get clipped.

Love

8. Give your dog lots of hugs.

9. Talk to your dog whenever you can.

10. Correct your dog's bad behaviours right away.